ASCENT

ASCENT

LUDWIG HOHL

translated by

DONNA STONECIPHER

BLACK SQUARE EDITIONS

2012

Bergfahrt by Ludwig Hohl
copyright © 1975 Suhrkamp Verlag, Frankfurt am Main
Translation copyright ©2012 Donna Stonecipher

COVER IMAGE:
Staircase to Heaven, 1977
Painting by Helmut Federle
Copyright © Helmut Federle and Pro Litteris, Zürich

DESIGN: Shari DeGraw

ISBN: 978-0-9860050-1-5

BSE BOOKS ARE
DISTRIBUTED BY SPD:
Small Press Distribution
1341 Seventh Street
Berkeley, California 94710

1-800-869-7553
orders@spdbooks.org
www.spdbooks.org

CONTRIBUTIONS TO
BSE CAN BE MADE TO:
Off The Park Press
73 Fifth Avenue
New York, New York 10003

(*please specify your donation
is for Black Square Editions*)

TO CONTACT THE PRESS, PLEASE WRITE:
Black Square Editions
1200 Broadway, Suite 3C
New York, New York 10001

An independent subsidiary of Off The Park Press

ASCENT

I

AN IMMENSE SHIP

In early summer, in the earliest morning hour, deep in the Alps, at the meeting point of two valleys, on green iron chairs in front of a still-sleeping café sat two figures, from their appearance and equipment not difficult to recognize as alpinists (thick woolen clothing and felt hats, rucksacks, a coiled rope over the one long pickaxe, and heavy nailed shoes — the story takes place in one of the early decades of the century). They were waiting for a bus that would take them a ways higher into the neighboring valley. Tall and gaunt the one, with a sleepy expression on his face; and after a time he really did fall asleep. The other, not nearly as tall, of a more concentrated character, looked incessantly up, looked searchingly up, to the summits of some of the mountains, how they stood all around with an unusually powerful, radiant presence.

"If only he would come with me!" he murmured barely audibly – or perhaps he only thought it – of his sleeping companion.

The flat valley, cut deep into the high mountains, had reached the apotheosis of its fertility; here and there a meadow had already been mown, while the others awaited their reapers, a manifold sea of towering green. How many know what magic a fertile mountain valley can unfold on a very early morning of this season and in very good weather; a magic that contains all at once something powerful, something ineffably tender, and something ominous? The power comes from the wealth of green, the immensity of the mountains, the light of the sky, which is so big that the sky can't yet be blue; its future blue waits behind a brightness, a shifting, shimmering white, the color of pewter (the sun shines first on the highest mountains, not here for a long time yet). The tenderness, on the other hand, the quiet, the ineffable quality, comes about through a trace of fog in the lowlands, the sound of a scythe that sometimes arrives from some distant place, the deep peace of the valley. Out of the depths of all kinds of green, the little river flashes here and there, full of promise, violent. – One of the two little rivers, to be precise, that somewhere near here, hidden between light-green bushes, meet.

For it is two valleys we are overlooking, the terrain is vast. And in an immeasurably wide pedestal the mountain mass rises out of the two valleys, and one is forced to gaze upon it, above all other things: dark with forests, then, at higher levels, secured by peaceful walls, sometimes slopes made of debris, then out of new cliffs, finally out of glaciers, it rises up to the highest ridge, very elongated, that ends abruptly in an almost vertical break, and that, joining several peaks, without a struggle, without a flaw, before the bright, glimmering bright background, sweeps in, exhibiting the greatest contrast to this fissured, wild, bizarre mountain range.

This is how, from a certain distance and from below, the mountain is seen. It is only steepness, cool victory, unquestionable victory. The highest part of its face of névé and gray, lightly shining, flat rock, looks like a shield, a suit of armor, a work finely inlaid in silver or steel. And the whole elongated form of this summit before the bright sky might also have awakened the impression of a very large ship, that is sailing not only into an earthen sea, but into eternity.

2

FIRST ASCENT

In the morning they completed the first stage of the ascent, through the sparse mountain woods along a serpentine path, over a long and steep slope, through which light and air flowed, and which stood in both the lingering coolness and also the first warmth. Ull went first, followed by the tall, gaunt Johann, but they did not proceed in the same manner: both were indeed bent over, but the first was bent to a slightly greater degree, and made lithe, almost careless movements; he was a good mountain-climber. The second, in contrast, had nothing lithe about him; he was exerting himself, as if he needed to strike the mountain with hard blows: a bad climber.

Soon they had broken out in a light sweat; the leather straps of their heavy rucksacks were pinching, a spot in their shoes was pinching, at their belts or somewhere else. In the steady sound of the scratching nailed shoes, the tip of the pickaxe on the stone and the rolling till, in the fact that they never seemed to get any higher, the laborious hiking up the path resembled that of many others – of hundreds of others. Out of the deep: the murmur or soft roar of a brook, now barely audible, now more so. One hour, two hours long, more – and it seemed that the ascent would go on forever.

But all at once much had changed. The incline was at an end, had given way to a kind of broad shoulder, which protruded at a right angle to the incline against the entire mountainside, lightly ascending. The sparse wood had now disappeared; most noticeably, its deciduous trees were replaced more and more by fir trees, and these stood only scattered and meager in meadows; they began to enter the region of the alpine pastures.

They had already got a thousand meters under them. A broad view had opened up. They sat down to rest next to a spring on the path, a little waterway that ran over rocks in the midst of a wide swathe of grass that crossed the path, ascending in a zigzag, against the base of a larger and connected cliff wall, which, a little higher up, displaced the meadow slopes. It had gotten warmer, slope and rock radiated a real heat, there was no wind, and a miraculous peace spread over everything. The mountain grass all around, of a bitter green, harder and tenderer and shorter than the thick grass of the valleys, invited one to rest. They looked down into the upper part of the side valley, at its small river and, beyond that, a little higher, at a veritably dreaming hamlet, it looked so still, so pure, resting in such a noble peacefulness, as no hamlet in reality could – if you want to call reality that nearness where you can live with a thing, touch it. And the sound of the brook or small river – or perhaps still other, different brooks – rose incessantly up, hushed and melodious, out of the deep. But always here above, next to the soft grass-cushions bejeweled with delicate flowers, the beautiful, eternally quiescent cliffs, some in bluish-blackish shadows, others glittering, almost trembling under the force of the midday sun, emitting a quivering light.

"We have time; we can stay here an hour or two if we feel like it." Ull had opened his rucksack, taken a few things out of it. Johann had also set his rucksack down, sat next to it, and did not move. Ull handed him a cup of clear water, which he immediately emptied and gave back, and then once again sat motionless. "Don't you want to eat anything?"

"I'll eat when we're up there."

"Where 'up there'? What the devil do you mean by that? Maybe in the hut — maybe tomorrow on a peak?"

A shrug of the shoulders instead of an answer.

"You know that for a mountain-climber it's very important to take nourishment, and right from the start."

He wanted to add: "If you don't eat anything now, you won't make it," but he held his tongue.

It should, however, be noted that in his regular life Johann was a big eater, despite his gauntness. In Paris in a little restaurant he would, not rarely, order two *menus* at once with only one place setting; in the afternoon he'd buy three hundred grams of cheese which he would cut up into approximately twenty cubes and wolf down with an appropriate amount of bread. On the preceding day, as they were walking through the market gathering provisions, he had eyed cans containing a kilo of beef; but Ull had advised him against it (because such cans can't be eaten up in one sitting, but also can't be kept, thus presenting an unnecessary burden); afterward it came out that he had smuggled along three such cans. When Johann suffered from a bout of melancholy, which happened often, it did not tend to diminish his gluttony – quite the opposite. That's why Ull was now worried. He tried again to cajole him. And again the answer:

"When we're up there."

At the same time he waved his hand in a helpless gesture at the immense, vast, towering mountainside.

3

IN THE ALPINE HUT

The first and most modest rock shelf on the easy path was quickly overcome; it formed the threshold to a perfectly flat, elongated terrace, the actual alp. Here everything was different! The view into the lowlands, into the inhabited world, was all of a sudden cut off; there were still extended fields of winter snow, next to bare patches that looked like faded cushions, but there were also some greener fields, on which a profusion of snowdrops were springing up. Somewhere there were three alpine huts. The pasture was naturally not yet inhabited at this time of year; there was no sign of humanity anywhere. (Just as they had encountered no sign of humanity on the entire climb since they left the last hamlet, aside from the path and a small hay shack.) And it was cool, because the sun no longer shone on the north slope in the afternoons, at least where a giant rise set in — as here, just after the narrow terrace — some six hundred meters high, made up of all sorts of cliffs, but especially between snow and snow.

Ull stood still and looked up, peering intently, and finally shook his head.

"You see — you see there, about halfway up the slope, the black, almost exactly triangular rock face? The hut must be at its foot, I'm sure I'm right — I mean the shelter that we were to quarter in tonight." But all one could see, at the designated spot, was an unbroken expanse of snow.

Ull continued: "I knew the summer was late in coming this year, but *so* late —. Well, the shelter has either disappeared — been burned or pulled down — or it's completely buried under the snow."

They hiked over the plateau to look at the alpine huts, which lay at a distance of about two minutes from one another. The first was locked up; the second was a ruin; the third might possibly be suitable for a stay. Below, a stall, the floor covered in cow dung, otherwise completely barren; above, however, there was a loft with a sufficient amount of hay — and even a supply of wood. Its entrance was reached from outside, on the side opposite the stall door, by just two stone steps: for the hut had been built into an incline, against an overhanging elongated ridge (not difficult to recognize as an old moraine). From this fact inhered a certain import for the stay in the hut, because while the hayloft had a solid roof, it had no real walls: the upright boards didn't connect up, but had gaps in between them roughly equivalent to their own width. An import, thus, as to its capacity to protect them from the wind. — And, as is almost always the case with alpine huts, water flowed nearby.

"What do you think?" Ull began again. "I think it'd be better if we stayed here. Remaining here overnight has its advantages and disadvantages. Tomorrow's climb will be an hour longer. But it will probably be impossible to get the door free, maybe even just to find the shelter. And there we definitely won't have water or any way to make a fire. If we climb up there now, we risk doing so for nothing, and having to come back here anyway to sleep."

Johann had no objection.

"I advise you to follow my example," Ull said, as, still early in the evening, they proceeded to get ready for bed. "First you make a pit in the hay, as you see here, as narrow and deep as possible, meaning the sides of the hay should be close to each other and as high and steep as possible. At the top of the pit, your rucksack for a pillow. Then the blanket over you." These were very meager blankets, which they had taken to use in any circumstances, not large and, most importantly, not heavy. "When you're stretched out in your pit, all you need is a few movements to make the hay fall over your body; you're buried so deep that you won't freeze, even if it gets colder."

Johann did not follow his example.

He did not at all have a good night. Ull woke up a first time: he heard noises; someone was feeling around in the dark.

"Are you looking for something?"

"Oh," Johann answered in an irritated and almost tearful voice, "it's the wind, it's making a whistling sound through a hole again. I've got to block it."

Later Ull woke up again: Johann was once more making noise, a board was moved, a soft groan could be heard; called to, he answered in a voice similar to the one from before: no, it wasn't the same hole, now the wind was whistling so miserably through another hole!

"But the entire wall is made up of holes! Do bed down in the hay as I showed you!"

Meanwhile the night was almost completely still, and one could hardly speak of a whistling wind. To be sure, from time to time one could hear a large, faraway rushing as if from the sea, long and drawn out, as if from an enormous bellows that moved slowly of its own accord, intakes of breath, as if someone sleeping were mildly sighing — a sleeper, but not of the small size of an animal or a human being: the mountain range itself was perhaps this sleeper.

Then again came the general stillness of the mountain night, that vast stillness whose base, however, is made up of an endless, melodious roaring, but a roaring so soft that you can no longer hear it as soon as the least other noise arises, and then afterward is once again there, mysterious and unchangeable, as if from giant faraway kettles that you would never find if you went looking for them.

20

4

DREAM OF THE BEAR

Once, Ull went out of the hut to scout out the weather — a few signs the previous evening had made him anxious — and lo! the entire sky was overcast.

Every time Ull woke up (only to go immediately back to sleep), he found Johann also already awake, he heard him quietly sighing, groaning, murmuring. To conclude from this, however, that on this night Johann had not slept at all would be incorrect, which is evident from the fact that Johann had had a dream that seemed to him so important that, the next day, breaking his usual silence, he related it in detail to Ull:

He found himself in an alarming — in the most alarming of situations. For what he was faced with, what threatened him, was nothing other than a bear, and not a small one, not a tame or a caged one, but a freely roaming and very large bear, whose sweet facial expression could not conceal his intentions, his frightening power. Johann felt himself from the first moment as if too annihilated, too paralyzed, to take any effective action, or even just to try to. But there was another person with him; there were two of them to take on the villain. This other person was a friend from high school, in those days the best mathematician in the class, a dry, peculiar person who liked to explain everything from a mathematical perspective. He did not seem to be intimidated by the appearance of the bear, but explained a complicated method by which one would confront the bear and become its master, got excited explaining and proving the parts of the method; he behaved exactly like a chess player who, rather than playing himself, demonstrates didactically to someone else an unusual move or an entire tactic, selfless, fascinated by the details and thinking less of victory than of the splendor of the warfare. It was all wonderfully thought through, to be sure, but it exerted upon the doings of the unpredictable and uncanny fellow not the slightest influence. — Then Ull arrived.

He just laughed. (He was wearing his peculiar, somewhat sarcastic, grin, which at times could change with astonishing suddenness into an expression of the most intense concentration.) He looked almost inconspicuous, seemed even smaller than usual. But what a charge, what certitude radiated from his person! Just in the way he strode up to the bear, you knew that the bear's fate was sealed. Small and grand, he stood before the bear like an ivory figurine, totally overwhelmed in height and width; the bear, however, had become like a giant piece of cloth, utterly will-less; he sank his head, abashed, into his plump bulk. And where Ull indicated to him to go with nothing but a nod, the bear went.

5

THE MELANCHOLY-SLOPE

Since, in the early morning hours, a decisive rain had already set in, Ull saw himself relieved of the difficult task of weighing whether setting off for a climb was advisable or not advisable; and it looked as though it would rain or snow all day; thick fog covered the immediate surroundings almost without reprieve.

Such a day of waiting in the mountains is long, and yet usually not so long as one might assume. As one is denied any prospect or possibility of influencing the future, one is forced to turn to the nearby and usual things, things so small and close that up to now they have almost always been overlooked, and one makes unusual discoveries. The things in the rucksack take on new life (for example, a thread and a needle, to sew on a button); also the various stones in front of the hut, among which one chooses the one best suited (or rather, the two best suited) to secure a loose nail back onto a shoe; from under the threshold comes a strange little beetle eager to devote itself to some for us incomprehensible activity; and when everything is very still and you don't move, you will, after a while, surely catch a glimpse of a mouse. The nearby knolls and boulders of an old moraine, otherwise completely unnoticed and now, in the fog, forming the outermost edge of the world, assume a face of varied character. And when one is well stocked with provisions and tobacco, it is not rare that, on such days, there unfolds a peculiar delight. The source of memory opens; and then mountain-climbers break their silence — good alpinists are almost always taciturn — and recount in detail what they otherwise never find the time or the self-possession of their gaze for: past, often in the distant past, journeys, moments splendid and (far more likely) menacing, difficult hours or quarter-hours they survived, that, sure enough, have now also already become splendid… Even Ull would have liked to do this; but every attempt failed thanks to the state of his listener — who in fact was by no means a listener at all. For how should one speak to a figure made of wood or plaster? Johann was looking somewhere — where? No, he was looking nowhere. Not a breath of inner life emanated from him.

But suddenly he caught a glimpse of something; his face came to life; his eyes grew transfixed, were actually spellbound. He was looking in a mirror:

Namely, once in the course of the darkened day a window formed in the cloud-masses, through which one looked upon the faraway slope of a high valley, which appeared at first to be a nondescript slope, bare and desolate. Immeasurable billowing fogs receded on both sides, knotting and unknotting, peacefully flowing and lengthening. What one could see, framed in this manner, was a completely monotonous, vast terrain made of steep pastures, or rather a large piece of it, because it was disappearing into the fog toward the top and the other three sides. In an almost regular fashion, this dull valley slope was crossed by numberless fine gray or yellowish threads: brooks, fed by the rain; in its entire expanse it showed no abrupt cliff, no ravine, no other sensation for the eye: its monotony was complete; in its olive-green, gray-green color, in the unimaginably dull light, which it more and more let dissolve into the detailed, the spun, the fine, it had truly taken on the imprint of infinity: and in this monotony, dullness, and endlessness, it nevertheless appeared to attain a greater effect at this hour than the pointiest, boldest jags, the most serene crests ever could have, was more gripping in its expression of tenderness and inexpressible darkness, its wistful loneliness, and truly infinite melancholy. No one paid any attention to this valley wall in good weather, it had only ever been a slope, a connection, by no gaze considered as anything else, for every gaze rushed quickly up to the edges, the jags, the sky; but now all at once it had been given a voice owing to a great hardship of weather, and the crests had fallen silent.

6

EARLY START

It is not child's play, getting up at two or three in the morning, the hour at which one usually sleeps most deeply, in such a dark hut, with the wind rushing through it, in the midst of such a totally inhospitable mountain night; the mountain night, which makes everything more uncanny than ever, in which the mountain becomes a boundless dark mass, in reality not unlike those demonic dream-figures that plague even very experienced, during the day very self-assured, alpinists, in half-sleep on such nights. The darkness of the hut intensifies the impression of cold, and even when one manages, after much painstaking feeling around and many failed attempts, to light the candle in the lantern, this wavering little light, which makes giant, moving shadows spring up all around, can't produce the feeling of greater warmth. One could say that such a lantern makes mainly shadows, not light; and the shadows move, because one must keep changing the location of the lantern, because people move, because the lantern, when it is hung up, swings, and finally because of the flickering of the flame. Only in a narrowly defined space does its glow let one recognize anything clearly, one must painstakingly gather all one's little objects together. To the cold is added, to intensify one's discomfiture, an increased feeling of uncleanliness; there will always be blades of hay sticking to one, and these blades of hay are dusty, short, and serrated; all over one's clothing they stubbornly attach themselves, and one must pick them off one by one by hand; but they have also burrowed under clothes, into sleeves, in the nape of one's neck; they are even in one's hair. So in the darkness and the cold he who has just gotten up feels tempted to make absolutely no movement, to keep his hands in his pockets, his body held tightly together. For if he engages in any unconsidered motion, he will certainly knock his head on a beam or step into one of the never-absent holes between the floorboards. Once he finally gets the door open, the door that unfailingly makes excessively loud creaking or groaning noises, but now and then is also ripped out of his hand by the wind to bang against the other side, so at his first glimpse of the mountain-world—glassy-uncanny, when the moon is shining, and otherwise murky-uncanny—the feeling of cold will without exception be still greater, even when in reality it was not any less cold in the hut.

Since this getting-up counts to a certain degree as one of the difficulties of the climb, the leader usually assumes his role already here: it is he who gets up first, wakes up the others and, inasmuch as there is the possibility of it, takes over the preparation of a warm breakfast. Ull had sat up with the first faint sounds of the alarm—a pocket watch—but needed to waste no effort in waking his companion, for the latter lay, as the candle burned, already awake, his eyes wide open; he rose immediately and then sat there, after he'd put on his shoes, unmoving. He found nothing to occupy himself with, and also displayed not the least curiosity to look out at the weather. Taking the lantern with him, Ull now went with a small pot down into the stall, there to prepare a hot drink on a stove erected on the previous day with stones and with wood that was also lying at the ready. When it was prepared, he held it out first to Johann. "Have some! This drink will give you the strength of a giant." (Joking didn't come very easily to him.) Johann accepted the drink with obvious pleasure, but then didn't seem to think of eating anything. Ull felt forced to talk him vigorously into it: it was imperative, he must force himself, etc., for otherwise it was very likely that during the first hours of the climb, nausea would set in.

After the meal he hung up a part of the things that they were going to leave there on a rope from the ceiling in the very middle of the room and explained that it must be done because one must always beware of mice and rats.

"Rats," said Johann. It was his first word of the morning.

Ull was the first to go out, in order to have a look around in the beginning day before they set off; standing again on the old moraine, he called in a loud voice, "It's still drizzling a little, but the air is excellent, glacier air, soon everything will be shining!" And at the same time he brought the steel tip of his pickaxe down forcefully on a stone. — Then he saw Johann's head, ghostly, look out through a gap in the door boards.

At the unexpectedly sudden, bright sound of the human voice from outside, from whence otherwise one heard only completely different, muffled sounds, Johann had winced. Now he went out into this world, where the night and the morning fog-waves battled each other; the wind that received him was icy. And after a few steps, when he turned back to look at the hut, it was already a body apart, and had already begun, now only the color of steel, to become a cold colossus, like one of those boulders. The last coziness — for a certain coziness, it only now became clear, had existed in the hut — had disappeared; one was exposed.

The wind was icy, and the weather, no, one couldn't call it good! Thick clouds that were growing ever more gray and blue-black hung down deeply; the cold slopes all around, whose details began to be more sharply visible, massive and brazen nearby, on both sides losing themselves up in the marvelousness of ravines and distance, disappeared up into dark, smoky, severe gray fog; there was no clear view of anything at a great height: and yet everything was waiting up there, cliffs and glaciers and crashes, dark chimneys, frightful storms, unspeakable exertions…

Only directly above them could they see pieces of the sky, pale and remote, with a star that had grown thin; and the dark mass of the mountain, vanishing in the brewing enormous clouds, climbed to that height; and no ridge was free of fog up there, in front of a bright piece of sky, with a few jags, that called. The giant rock-bodies of the mountain, which had joined forces with infinity, were stored there, the whole world was a smoking cauldron, inhuman and horrifying, and Ull's voice was the only thing that called.

7

ASCENT TO THE SHELTER

The alpine terrace was crossed quickly, and now they began to tackle the large, multiform, composite mountainside. At first Ull followed a faint path, which quickly vanished under snow; soon they were climbing constantly over snow. (In flat grooves and on bands between rock faces of various sizes.) The terrace sank quickly into the depths; it grew even more level than it had been — perfectly level. And now the light of the beginning day was reflected on this plateau in a singular way: numerous tiny streams (which one hadn't noticed, from below), frozen flat pools, and finally also the snowy fields stood out against the dark ground, like various circular cut metal plates; some of these platinum or tin plates were perfectly matte, with curved edges of unimaginable fineness and sharpness; others were extraordinarily bright, sending out an intense light without any tint, without any vibration, without the least trace of a warm shine; its bright, violent shine discharged all its light at once and thus it was, even if shine and brightest shine, nevertheless of an inexorable hardness. These frightening mirrors (in which nothing was reflected) had this unbrokenness, this untinted closedness, in common with the other metal fittings, the matte ones. Now if one were to imagine an innumerable quantity of both kinds — especially the meandering forms of the many-branched little streams — and that they were all bound and held in a wonderfully harmonized dark ground — then one would get a faint idea of what treasures of incomparable richness this plateau, sunk in the deeps, displayed in the cold beginning daylight.

But the weather — no, it wasn't good; still not and despite Ull's prediction; they could see the plateau under them, yes, but not much else; all around the clouds were stowed in heavy masses; and even now from time to time the wind still drove a flock of fine snowflakes at them.

After a hike of about an hour, Ull changed direction; he crossed a less steep snow field in a horizontal line, against the foot of a sharply emerging dark cliff (whose triangular shape no longer existed at such close range) and moved along the almost flat snow only hesitantly; then he finally thrust the shaft of his pickaxe deep in the snow.

"Hear that?"

Johann looked up: "No."

He thrust the pickaxe in the ground again, and several more times, and finally Johann heard the muffled sound.

Ull gave a short laugh. "We're standing on the roof."

"…But there's no way to get inside?" He spoke hesitantly, half-aware of the senselessness of the question.

"Stay here. The roof is flat, or only slightly slanted, and on the mountain side merges into the slope, if I remember correctly. The entrance faces the valley, so we must be careful there, where the roof projects."

He moved in this direction, constantly sounding with the pickaxe, as one tends to do on a snow-covered glacier full of crevasses. And lo, suddenly there was a hole in the snow, which could only be seen from up close; but the bulging edge made of soft snow was easily widened, and now one could see into a hollow leading steeply downward, which spread out below, and there, in the half-dusky light under the broadly projecting roof, one recognized part of a door.

Ull got into the hole first, after having laid aside his rucksack; he managed to pull open a latch and by kicking the door to make it give way, and then he slid completely into the hut. Johann followed.—A musty, tomb-like twilight.

A candle was quickly found and lit. A single, fairly large bed, sufficient for several persons, took up most of the space. Then there was also a table and, most important, an old thing that was both oven and stove. What was definitely missing: water and wood. And whether the chimney could be got free remained to be seen.

Their rest would not last long.

8

ASCENT TO THE GLACIER

In the next part of the ascent, moving forward proved quickly to be difficult, because the snow got deeper and especially – surprisingly, considering how high up they were and the time of day – softer; they often sank in up to the tops of their shoes. So one hour passed and almost another hour, till finally the slopes got rounder and receded; the great mountain inclines were overcome and a new plateau reached, parallel with the alpine terrace, but situated approximately seven hundred meters higher. Because of the extraordinary effort that the climb had cost them, they had barely noticed the weather; now, however, hardly had they reached the edge of this terrace than it forced them with the utmost insistence to pay attention: the almost unbroken wind sweeping over the white surface was so fierce and merciless that for the present they could think only of it.

They should have stopped, but where? At the edge of the plain there were still a few low rocks rising out of the snow; but there was not one among them, as far as the eye could see, whose leeward side was steep and high enough to offer a bit of shelter. So Ull, postponing their rest,

pushed on.

But not without first having cast a glance (as far as it was possible, between two gusts of wind) at the summit of the mountain, which here was again partly visible, for the first time since they had sat in front of the little café in the green valley, and which still towered above them a full thousand meters. But how different it looked here! One could no longer speak of a fine silver-work; the rocks now proved themselves to be a stormy confusion of jagged pillars, ribs, towers, dark grooves, steep sloping gorges; everything, except for the perfectly vertical rocks, powdered over with new snow (from the previous day and the night before that). As for glaciers, only one was visible from here, and indeed only its topmost part — and its bottommost, where it ended above a house-high vertical cliff in a maze of those bizarre figures that one calls, in the alpinist's language, seracs. (They were waiting there so that, when their hour was come, one after the other, they would burst and collapse.)

The seracs: A glacier is a river of ice that is moving, slowly. Because, however, its bed never runs regularly, at those places where a sharp descent sets in (and where the water of a regular river would foam), fissures form — the usual crevasses, which extend at right angles to the general direction of the glacier. But the ground can also sink to the side, and that means that cracks rupture running at right angles to the first ones, so that a number of rectangles and squares come into being (and this is only a general pattern, the reality is naturally more complex). One can speak of a crevasse-confusion — not yet at all of a serac; of a crevasse-confusion, which is perhaps a preliminary phase out of which seracs can develop, when several circumstances work together in a way that is difficult to fully understand.

To be sure, a few insignificant crevasses are to be found on every glacier; and on most glaciers there are sections of myriad dangerous cre- vasses; true seracs, however, are relatively rare — indeed, in fact, because very particular conditions are necessary for them to come into being. Out of a number of squares and rectangles, slabs and cubes are the first to form; how so? It is as if the glacier were chopped up, it is the custom to say. (Who chopped it up?) The slabs predominate; in a later phase one could speak rather of towers and towerlets, though towers not at all uniform, neither equally tall, nor necessarily upright, but of every imaginable shape. They can be two or three meters, but also, in exceptional cases, ten meters tall; they can have bulging, but also con- cave sides; they can end at the top in a point, but also in a wide head, hanging so far over that one expects them to collapse (and, sooner or later, they do collapse). What could have hewn the glacier in this way? The underground terrain, the rock ground that one cannot see, must doubtless be responsible for much of it; likewise the sunshine, which melts the blocks mostly from one side, at which point the water runs underneath, thereupon to freeze again; the block's own weight, vertical to the earth; the traction of the glacier in its lengthwise direction: to find a mathematical formula for the interworking of all of these — and certainly more — conditions, one can turn only to the devil himself, and even he probably wouldn't be able to come up with it. One cannot explain it, the seracs are simply there: they exist! It also occasionally happens that one comes upon a great number of figures, all nearly alike, not tall, and parallel, and for a moment they look like a herd of cattle;

but mostly they are in every respect as unalike as can be. Where is the surface of the glacier and what is it like? Difficult to say. It's there and not there. One can't in any case speak of a single surface. Here, at the foot of a giant tower, is an attached cornice — but only two steps wide, then it ends in a hole perhaps ten meters deep. There one sees clearly how one of the figures rests on a pillar that shoots down into the unfathomable; while another figure appears to merge below into a safe snow-slope; which, however, seen from another side, turns out to be only a thin layer of snow over an extremely weak ice vault, under which there is nothing but emptiness to a great depth, where presumably something similar is repeated. One can even sometimes hear brooks rushing in the depths. — For the glacier is "chopped up" not only from above; from the side, too, it is fragmented into all kinds of vaults, chambers, floors, similar to the foundations, many stories deep, of a destroyed factory; and if, by a miracle, one managed to see into the darknesses of this substructure, what one would see there would surely resemble certain etchings by Piranesi.

But up above, these crippled, up-stretched figures are of the most extreme variety; here crookedly posed, there soaring like flames, some so tilted that one asks oneself how they can continue to stand, others massive and hulking, some standing at a distance from each other, others, most of them, close together — dreadful and grotesque at the same time; a tumult of figures or forms, like matterhorns or vampires' teeth, an arrangement of lions or bears, caricatures of a baker or miller's boy with his sack on his back, an alderman with a black hat, a mourning woman hung with cloths from head to toe, of crocodiles and dragons.

— Ull pointed to the cliffs, over which the seracs had appeared.

"Horrible!" Johann burst out.

The best actor in the world could not have uttered the word with more expressive power.

9

They crossed the plateau not toward the rock face, of course, but far to the side of it, in a big loop over moderately inclined slopes, in order to gain access to the glacier above the seracs. The wind picked up. Ull helped Johann to secure his hat in the same way that he had just secured his own as they went along; that is, the brim on both sides completely pulled down, with a large handkerchief run under the chin, its ends tied up over the crown of the head. And Ull stopped several times, he uncoiled the rope. Johann watched these precautionary measures with signs of uneasiness.

"Is this the glacier?"

"Not yet, presumably. We won't notice it starting under us. I'm doing this to be on the safe side; farther up, putting on the ropes might be more uncomfortable."

He bound Johann fast to the rope on one end, tied himself in the middle, and led the other half again to Johann, so that they were doubly bound — as is necessary when you cross a glacier as a pair. He gave Johann some more instructions.

A half hour went by, during which they climbed on with difficulty, first keeping to the right, then, somewhat steeper, straight upward, then, to close the curve, again to the left on less steep ground, which slowly became almost flat. (It was the level of the glacier above the seracs.) Ull's task was growing harder, not so much because he had to watch out for any crevasses (which would not be considerable here), but because it became ever more difficult to orient himself in the growing snowstorm. Occasionally, for a short time, a window opened, the foot of the universal cliff wall appeared, a tower in a swirl of snow, a steep gorge, a rise of the glacier — and Ull had to decide which way to go based on them.

For it had become a real snowstorm; it raged with such force that the wind that had swept over the plateau now seemed harmless by contrast. It lifted large amounts of powdery snow into the air and chased it about in clouds — clouds that had little in common with the usual kind; they had nothing mild and enveloping about them, but, made of fine, hard kernels, hit their bodies with such violence that in spite of their being bundled up in thick clothing, they felt at times as if they were exposed naked to the lashing ice needles.

It hindered their breathing. One had to push against it. They pressed forward bent over, using the pickaxes as staffs. Their sight was so limited that they mostly saw nothing of each other (from the distance of about thirteen meters; the entire rope was thirty meters long). Then again a kind of form was recognized, but without precise attributes, so rather only a phantom. Calling to each other was out of the question, because no words would be understood.

So the little party pressed forward through the snowstorm, slowly, to be sure, but yet unvanquished, if also with little hope — through the wilderness of this white night, which surrounded them, roaring, booming, and clattering.

IO

TURNING BACK

But now something else happened; the rope grew taut and made further forward motion for Ull impossible. Certainly, the storm was straining the rope (even though it was only a centimeter thick), so that it bound the two of them mostly in a slight curve, and for the first climber represented a burden that had to be, in some sense, towed; but now this resistance had suddenly grown much greater; even a few strong tugs had no effect. Had Johann fallen into a crevasse? In that case a stronger pull backward would have occurred and, anyway, here the crevasses were — if there were any at all — very narrow and shallow. Had he twisted his ankle, or was he maybe even lying back there unconscious on the ground? In any case — what choice did he have but to turn back, to see what had happened to Johann?

So he went backward, collecting the rope in loop after loop, and soon he perceived a figure that appeared to be gesticulating; that is to say, had its arms raised (and was probably screaming something at him). Then they stood face to face, two strange, mummylike, equally awkward and disheveled forms, covered over and over with scales of ice.

"Neck," was the first word that Ull understood.

"What, neck?"

"There — pain — in my neck. And my back hurts. And also my chest — breathing."

Ull searched Johann's face, as far as was possible between the pulled-down sides of the hat. He really did look miserable.

"I can't anymore. — Can't go on."

Now Ull stood a while in front of Johann without speaking, very much like a doctor who, after the examination has ended and the questions have been asked, looks half-absently at the patient, striving to form a precise picture of the difficulty from what he has just learned. He could not take Johann's symptoms of malady or infirmity seriously.

But other considerations pressed in: the chances of a successful summit were now extremely low — even apart from the state of his companion; for eight o'clock had already come and gone and the storm showed no signs of letting up — on the contrary. Here one could still progress, but when, soon, the glacier began to rise, with giant crevasses, with all sorts of difficulties, with extremely exposed places — then a further forward movement in such weather was out of the question. Johann was not ill, but he was exhausted, he was discouraged; was it worth it to encourage him, to rouse him, to try, with all his personal powers, to convince him to go on (apart from the fact that talking in the snowstorm was extremely difficult) — only, with nine-tenths probability, to have to give up the summit in another half hour anyway? And also, considering the next few days: was it smart to try to sway Johann now, already, or to ask too much of him?

He gave the signal to turn around.

A bit farther down, as they took off the rope, Ull felt compelled to say: "It's not because of your complaints — they'll soon be past — but because reaching the summit today was hardly possible."

After they crossed the plateau, the descent over the slope, which had cost them so much effort during the ascent, was accomplished with extraordinary speed; they drove down through the soft snow sometimes sliding and sometimes in great leaps; it was striking that Johann showed himself cheerful and dexterous. Little avalanches let loose here and there, irrelevantly. From moment to moment it grew warmer. The sun was shining! At around ten they had once more reached the buried shelter.

Testing the stove, or rather getting the chimney free, proved to be easy; a newspaper burned without inundating them with smoke. "Now we have to go back down to the alp."

"Is that necessary?"

"Of course it's necessary! First, to get the things we left there and bring them up here, and then to get water, but especially to get wood! Otherwise what would we do tomorrow morning — where would we get water?"

The meadows of the alpine terrace, free of the old snow, had already rid themselves of the new snow and refreshed the eye with their long since unseen green; it remains, each time, a singular and memorable occurrence, when, still early in the day, one has descended with great speed out of the zone of the high mountains and into the region of the alpine meadows. The peculiar effect it produces may come about due to the unusual state of the mind, intensified by the unusual state of the body after its great efforts; to the memory of getting up in the middle of the night, setting off so early; to what one experienced up there, which now all seems almost like a dream. One feels that the duration of time

the eyes saw no green was much longer than it really was, as if one had, all day long, seen nothing but snow, ice, and cliffs. — It was midday, the sun radiated heat, the angry, icy wind of the heights had here become a cool breeze, perceptible only in the shade. The mild air, the humming silence, the pleasant warmth had something truly miraculous about them, and all of the mountain ridges, come out of the clouds, stood around them in undreamt-of cheerfulness.

II

IN THE UNDERGROUND CHAMBER

At the earliest of hours Ull peeled off his ragged blanket, lit a candle, opened the creaking door, and climbed out through the hole to take a look around: the night was utterly still, the sky clear and starry.

He went back into the chamber to make a fire and, especially, to see to Johann, who was already sitting up, as the changed position of the candle indicated, there in the middle of the musty blanket, not moving.

"How are you?" Ull asked — and instantly regretted it.

"Bad, very bad," came the immediate answer. "I didn't sleep at all last night. I still feel it in my head, my neck, my back. I just can't take this dreadful icy wind anymore."

"The snowstorm is over. The wind has completely stopped."

"Yes, but it could start up again. I can't breathe in it. And then those horrible seracs!"

"But we go around them. And didn't we turn back when the snowstorm got too severe? — And haven't we gone climbing in Switzerland before?"

"Yes, but the mountains weren't so high. And I was younger back then."

"And now at your great age — ." (He was twenty-three.) "You're talking like a madman. — You see, even the fire noticed, it's gone out."

He set about to get it going again. But Johann remained sitting in the same position, unmoving. Unmoved. No more to be moved, through whatever means.

The fire — what had it noticed? It was only a sign, an echo of what he now felt: that his power over Johann had come to an end.

Now the fire burned brightly. But this time it corresponded to another fire: that of an excessive fury, which began to fill him.

"So you want to just give up, you want to drop the whole thing?"

Out of a tomb-like silence, after a while:

"Yes."

Pause.

"And all your damned, deuced, imagined ailments, you really think — "

"You can mock me all you like, but I can't go on."

Now Ull began with rushed movements to get himself and his things ready to set off. So he was going to have to tackle the glacier alone — an almost insane undertaking; you almost certainly needed a companion, even if it wasn't a good companion. (For to be a safety, below, required no special talent. A person's weight alone could, under certain conditions, be enough, especially when this person was heavy, as Johann was.) Now he had to manage alone — the long effort to persuade Johann had come to nothing. He turned again to Johann, but only to scold him excessively, which Johann tolerated mutely, like a dog that has been hit, that knows it is guilty and that waits, meekly, for a kind of springtime.

Now he saw Ull go out, first pushing his rucksack up through the hole, then his pickaxe, then following himself, with the lantern; and it grew dark in the underground chamber.

But outside it was dark, too. The moon did not shine here, the mountain's gigantic shoulders hid it; without a lantern Ull would not have gone far; hardly had he gone a few steps from the shelter than the frozen snow-slope he had to climb up, there in the night, already demanded alertness, knowledge. Then a voice reached him; it was warmer, livelier than he had heard in a long time from Johann (who must have climbed at least partly out of the snow-hole); a good-bye and friendly wishes.

But Ull, in his fury, no longer answerered.

12

THE BATTLE WITH THE GLACIER

As day broke, Ull found himself approximately at the spot where they had turned back on the previous day, that is, on the glacier, before its first powerful rise. It is difficult to convey an impression of it. It's no longer seracs, but forms of a much larger size. Blocks as big as houses; next to one something like the entrance to a small valley, quickly turning, however, into scarps on all sides; there were also niches, terraces, but how would one reach them, and where would they end? Impossible to tell from here. Snow vaults, presumably hiding transverse crevasses — how wide and how deep? Scarps facing all sides. Finally, here and there an ice wall protruded from out of the tumult, vertical or overhanging, glistening greenish or bluish and mostly with its snow cap ending before the heavens. It's as if infinity had mistakenly thrust a shovel in there and thrown everything all around in confusion, and then left it lying wherever it had landed.

To master this approximately two-hundred-meter-high step of the glacier (which, farther up, was followed by another, similar one, after an almost level stretch — none of which, of course, could be seen from here), even an experienced rope team would have needed a lot of time. But one man, alone?

Ull had started out his climb to the summit in an excessive fury. And this fury still accompanied him; it was guiding him — more so than alpine wisdom.

On none of his previous ascents would he have done something like this.

The method that one person going it alone on such a glacier must use is very different from the method a rope team would use. Because for him there is no security, because if he falls into a crevasse he is lost, he must first examine every spot he will set his foot on very thoroughly with his pickaxe; further, and most important: many spots are out of the question from the start. To sum it up in a sentence: for he who goes it alone, the battle with the glacier lies much less in dealing with difficulties than in avoiding difficulties altogether.

But that demands a powerful stamina; indeed, it is, on such a glacier as this, an almost hopeless contest. Chasms lurk everywhere. He must avoid them with detours, either horizontally or going back down — with, apparently, endlessly detouring paths.

For example, he followed the bottom edge of a wide transverse crevasse for a while, and there at the end was a bridge, formed of a narrow ice-blade, that rose from the yawning depths; covered with snow above, approximately a foot wide and level, and leading over to a moderately steep slope that would have allowed him to easily climb at least twenty meters higher up. He examined this bridge from several positions. If he had been roped, he wouldn't have hesitated to take the path over the bridge, for the possibility of falling into a crevasse was small. Alone, he could not allow himself this risk. (Alpine wisdom had not yet completely deserted him; faced with one particular problem or detail, it was still there.) So he followed the crevasse farther, mostly on a kind of flat spine, almost to the edge of the glacier — where it slowly vanished and the glacier merged into cliffs in a manner difficult to define, cliffs of such smoothness and declivity that any thought of crossing them was ruled out. He succeeded, however, in the snow and ice, in reaching a spot approximately twenty meters higher; then nothing more was possible than to once again, now in the opposite direction and along the top edge, walk along the large crevasse in the hopes of finding, through the maze of steep slopes and ice figures, a new path upward. In doing so he passed by the bridge again — which, to be sure, he couldn't see, since a steep slope hid it; however, he clearly saw his own footprints (multiple, because he had hesitated), about thirty meters below him. Since he had been there, a whole hour had gone by; if he had crossed the bridge with a companion, they would have reached the same spot in about five minutes.

— Ull pushed on grimly. It did not occur to him that he should alter his plan. Certainly it would not have been easy to make a different choice. And from a certain height on, there was no escaping the glacier. Nevertheless, he could still have turned around, at least on the first part of the glacier, following his own tracks in the snow, which had not yet become soft. But he shrank in horror from the idea of perhaps encountering Johann again in the hut. He wanted nothing more to do with him!

The fury at Johann had turned into fury at the glacier. He had to reach the crest — and as for what came next, that would remain to be seen. He didn't think about it, he didn't want to think about it — but it accompanied him, darkly, anyway. Like that most eerie of dark feelings: to sense how the hours were slipping by…

13

ON THE CREST

The crest was reached, the glacier overcome! — And it was noon.

At first, exhaustion surpassed everything. He sat down, then lay down; there were ample opportunities to do so, on meter-wide horizontal pieces of dry stone between the last, still only slightly inclined, snow-slopes and the plunges of the south face.

A great warmth, indeed a heat, spread out in the hollow of the cliff. He had taken off his snow-goggles, had a sip of his water, stuffed some more snow into the canteen, and laid it beside him. And now, gradually calming down and at the same time coming to a more wakeful consciousness, he had to confess it fully to himself: he had fallen into a trap.

For, to go down the glacier, a glacier of this character, on now thoroughly soft snow and alone, was for today out of the question — it would have meant almost certain death. If, as foreseen in the original plan, he had ascended the summit on the right (over fairly difficult cliffs, from two to three hundred meters high) and then turned back again (the other routes to this summit were far longer and more difficult), the question would have remained unchanged: how to get down from the crest? To the left it continued a bit farther, perhaps a hundred meters, forming several gaps, on the whole horizontal and easy to cross; but then it rose into vertical, apparently unclimbable towers and ended God knows where. (Ull was lacking information on this, for back then no guidebook through this part of the Alps existed, at least none that he had been able to find; he'd had to arduously assemble what information he did have out of various publications.) — What remained was only the south face.

It looked horrific.

For one could see most of it from here, since it was, on the whole, concave; clearly visible at least was the uppermost and, except for an overhang following it, steepest part (about two hundred meters high). Where it was again visible under the overhang, it was significantly less steep and then got less and less steep to finally, more than one and a half thousand meters deep, give way to the top part of a high valley, of which one could see only a tiny piece.

This concavity of the south face stood in full opposition to the character of the north side, of the glacier, which was convex, and that means: from the crest one saw the snow-slope, which gradually grew steeper, and barely a hint, here or there, of the end of the last escarpment, but — nothing more; nothing more until, very far down and deep, green forests and meadows appeared, blooming valleys with little villages; beneath those, also indistinct, the place at the meeting-point of the two valleys where, three days ago, they had waited for the bus.

But another difference was more stupendous. When one looked

south: no human trace! Cliffs, snow, and ice. Black ridges, like stage sets one after the other, summits towering against the sky left and right and everywhere; farther down, gray rubble slopes, no other color, with the exception of that little spot at the end of the high valley, slightly greenish or yellowish, that one could briefly mistake for a flock of sheep — but not for long, for it did not move.

No human trace: not an upright pole nor a length of cable nor a footprint; not the slightest change to Nature such as (farther down) a little wall, a hut, a roof, a footbridge. A landscape out of prehistoric times. Had one stood there after the last ice age, fifteen thousand years earlier, exactly the same view would have presented itself.

And yet: a straight line, pulled through the air and the cliffs, only eight kilometers long, would have ended in the middle of a fat and lively village with around a thousand inhabitants! Here unthinkable, because in the high mountains distances have fully other values.

Midday was long gone; Ull was recovered from his exhaustion and yet not recovered; his thoughts ran to and fro, they went in wider circles, his focus shifted, and what emerged more and more, and finally, in all clarity: his girlfriend.

How could he have let her go away! With her by his side, he would not have fallen into this trap, and everything would have turned out differently. — She had expressed the urgent wish to go back to visit relatives of hers for a week in a city in the north; afterward she would come to the Alps and take Johann's place as his companion. He had given his consent. Yet if only he had asked, she would surely have given up her plans and come with him from the start.

Introduced to the mountains by Ull a few years earlier, she had quickly become a good alpinist. To be sure, she looked slight and thin, almost frail — but on long climbs brute strength is rarely important; chamois do not have the strength of oxen, but they are wonderful climbers. A longing for her took hold of him, a longing that quickly grew immeasurable. He felt compelled to call her name out loud — through cliffs and across plains, over hundreds of kilometers — and then the undertaking struck him as all too ridiculous. — Was his love for her greater than his love for the mountains? It was a different kind of love. He had the mountain now — or rather, it had him; it surrounded him, all around; in the all-powerful sunlight glittering, and in the darkness frozen stiff.

If a very reasonable and far-sighted spirit were to appear — that old man of the mountain, for example, that steps out of a cleft in the rock to protect the chamois, which is being hunted to death ("With his hand the Deity / Shields the beast that trembling sighs") — it would have given him the following advice: "Stay here, and in the evening bury yourself deep in the snow. Do not, so late in the day, undertake a descent down a rock face whose accessibility you know nothing about. Very early tomorrow, you will — if the weather doesn't change, but I can express to you my conviction that it will remain good — easily continue the descent over the glacier, in your tracks in the now-hard snow, which will still be there." But no spirit came out of a cleft in the rock.

And now, if you can believe it or not, something strange happened to him (to understand it, you must certainly not forget the physical fatigue as well as the lack of sleep during the past two days): He, hard as steel — in the eyes of others — the bear-tamer — in Johann's dream — stood on his crest, and sobbed.

14

THE SOUTH FACE

If I say, "The south face appeared as a singly monstrous precipice," I must then answer the question: what sense can it make today, to speak repeatedly of precipices, of nightmarish, horror-inspiring precipices? Today, when daily countless people, even old and frail people, whisk over countries and continents many thousands of meters high in the air? — The depths that one perceives from the windows of an airplane (if one even perceives them at all) are mostly an abstraction; the impression of an abyss, however, can only be produced through sensual perception. "We're flying at five thousand meters," the pilot announces. "You can see Bordeaux, the Gironde." When one of the sleepy passengers or businessmen buried in their documents takes the trouble to look down, as well as he can, he really does see Bordeaux, the Gironde — as on a map. But a map is an abstraction. For how often does it happen that, while looking at a map, one's head falls to the table from dizziness?

A ninety-year-old woman who is mostly paralyzed has just now flown over the continent and is asked how the flight was. "Thank you," she begins with a grousing voice. "Going up was fine. But coming down it almost took a bad turn, because there was an incompetent man at the

corner." An incompetent man — did she mean the copilot? No, actually, she was talking about going up and down the jetway in her wheelchair. — One looks down from the thirtieth floor and has no sensation of depth, or at least no trace of fear, the balustrade in front of the window is too wide, too sturdy; one sees a kind of garden area below, paths, a little house that at first one took for a rabbit hutch (there again, partly a map effect). If, however, you should walk on the gutter of an only one- or two-story house and this gutter is rusted and obviously no longer solid…the eight meters next to you seem like a kind of abyss. What can be concluded from all of this: for an alpinist, abysses never end.

— Ull, dreaming on his crest, finally recognized that he had to give himself a push (if life was to go on); and that meant that he must coax himself, exactly like another; as he had often coaxed others. Like, for example, his friend P., as P., standing before a notch in the crest, near the summit, had declared firmly: "There's no way I'm going over that. If you want to go on [they were three], untie me, I'm staying right here." The notch was what is called "razor-sharp," with chasms to left and right, but only one meter long; then the ridge rose up again, wide and in boulders one could get a good grip on. "But this is nothing. You can't give up now, a few meters before the summit." — "The abysses." — "Just don't look down. And anyway, you're secured on two sides. You're really going to regret it later if you give up the summit because of a completely unimportant little thing. Now, look!" And as if playing, he climbed the few meters down, placed a foot across the blade and one arm on the rocks lying across from it, and stretched the other into the air. Turning his face up and back: "You see? Not hard at all." He quickly climbed back up to the first ledge and – P. followed.

But it was incomparably more difficult to coax oneself. In addition: how different were the circumstances from those of the aforementioned case! P. could have waited, then turned back with the others on safe paths; Ull had no choice but to go on, and the only thing that offered itself as a path was the descent over the south face. – This was made up, in the uppermost and steepest part, almost exclusively of cliffs; but he – this is how he framed the argument, in order to extract from it the tools to convince himself – couldn't he consider himself a good, maybe even a very good, climber? Was that perhaps only his own opinion? No, there was clear evidence to the contrary. That northern ridge of Aiguille X, for example, which he had conquered alone, after only brief and incomplete verbal instructions – only to find out afterward, in guidebooks and from other people, that this climb was considered the most difficult of the entire area.

Now he set about to make the descent; immediately, for there was no way of knowing how much time he would need.

The only information he had found on the south face: a rope team had once scaled it with a guide from the Bernese Oberland, in the uppermost part through an ice couloir in which the guide had carved out four or five hundred steps. The couloir began in a gap about a hundred meters farther to the left in the ridge; using it for the descent was clearly out of the question.

The only possibility: the highest part of the face, almost completely free of snow, two to three hundred meters deep, had to be climbed along in an approximately straight line. This piece could be overseen.

But then the face (which in fact was only mostly concave) bulged out, into the air, only to be glimpsed again about a thousand meters deeper as an indistinct mix of expiring glacier, rock ridges, scree, ending in the aforementioned tiny piece of high valley.

64   Now he had to change direction, to the left, almost at a right angle to the left, to get to a passable area over a spot that likewise eluded his sight but was not long, against the aforementioned couloir that had to be crossed, now less steep and soon coming to an end. And the next step would remain to be seen.

The advance along the first, extremely steep part of the wall took much longer than expected; sidestepping and again sidestepping and starting again; small ridges or crests; tiny couloirs and flat troughs. And again, much time elapsed.

15

THE FIRST ACCIDENT

Not far from the large overhang, as he pulled down the rope and was gathering it in loops, while standing on a kind of small platform, that is where it happened — the incomprehensible.

He did not fall. But the pickaxe fell. And it was as if his friend, his only remaining friend, had abandoned him.

To lose the pickaxe — that is what cannot happen to an alpinist, and had never happened to him before. (The pickaxe, in those days, had a much more exclusive significance than it does today, when alpinists take a whole arsenal of small, mostly metal utensils with them on difficult climbs.)

Years ago, as he was preparing to stop for the night, he had arrived, very tired, high on a steep, frozen snow-slope, the end of which, far below him, he couldn't see; he had sat down briefly to rest and to think — and suddenly begun to slide; he couldn't stop, he slid faster and faster, then slower, and finally came to a halt where the snow-slope became almost level, between boulders. He had stood up with only mild injuries, which proved to be mostly abrasions on his hand – which, with an iron grip,

had held on to the pickaxe.

— But now it had happened. He had been carrying the pickaxe now in one hand, now in the other, now in a loop on his wrist. What force had interfered here, how could he have suddenly let it go? He wanted to chase after it, but of course that wasn't possible. The pickaxe tumbled and slid down, then disappeared, gave off a short cracking sound and, a bit later, reappeared again, already without its head, flung forth far from the mountain, indeed seemingly flying toward the sky, and then, after a sudden curve, it disappeared, soundlessly, forever.

16

THE TERRIBLE CLIFF

Now, to avoid the massive overhang, he moved along the wall more and more to the left, finally almost horizontally, and managed to reach the place where, in a now only narrow extension, the overhang joined an almost vertical pillar falling from the ridge. This was the only possible spot from which to continue this route; a piece of wall thirty or forty meters high that he hadn't been able to see from the ridge and that even now was still partly invisible.

He climbed ten meters straight upward without especial difficulties and reached a position that in these circumstances could be called comfortable: one foot with the entire sole set down, but one hand, no, the whole forearm, looped around a crag at chest or shoulder height, which, together with the wall, formed a notch that was wide at the top and narrow at the bottom. This position, which would have let him hold out as long as he wanted to without undue strain, gave him, at all events, the chance to survey the situation calmly — that is, as far as it could be surveyed.

First there was an extremely steep part, about three meters, and then — one saw nothing more; the overhang presided, and how high it was, could in no way be assessed; only about fifteen meters lower did the slope reemerge, now considerably less steep. The uppermost piece was provided with some tiny handles or steps, so tiny that one couldn't really call them that. With one exception: near the lower edge there was indeed a handle, and a mighty handle. It protruded from the stone like a wide sword. And immediately underneath it arched the hump, of which he could see only the beginning. And if this handle hadn't been there, he would have driven every thought of attempting to master this spot from his mind.

But what did he have a rope for, then, couldn't it be of some use? one might ask. The rope could have been of most excellent use here, could have solved all the difficulties — if he could have attached it. But that it was not possible to do. The notch in which his arm lay was out of the question, for at the slightest tug from below the rope would slip down into it, where it got narrower, and with further tugging it would get so stuck that there would be no way to get it loose again. (Even an elephant bound at one end could not have pulled it down, only ripped it apart.) The rope, therefore, could be of use only if one were to sacrifice it. (A single piton would have sufficed to remove these difficulties.)

Now there was, however, one more possibility: to use the rope for a first exploratory descent, and then to climb back up along the same path. Half of the rope should reach at least over the overhang, out into the passable area. Then, should descending without the rope seem humanly possible to him, he would take it out of the notch and continue the climb down without it.

However, considering the late hour, and also the large, sword-shaped handle, which in the worst case would allow him to climb back up again, he discarded this plan for a trial run; he risked it all.

He tied one end of the rope around his body; the other end to the rucksack and let it fall, first tumbling, then sinking into the invisible, then once more tumbling and again becoming visible about fifteen meters lower down, eventually sliding and frequently stopping, so that it needed a nudge from above to make it continue; finally it came to rest, to all appearances, in a kind of niche. – Ull was ready.

The first piece proved to be as difficult as it had looked. On the tiny stairs (which actually could not be called stairs, but what should one call them?) and with the help of the equally tiny handles, he climbed down with the utmost slowness. (To tackle a similar spot, albeit on the ascent and surrounded by gentle terrain, the guidebook instructions said: "Advance rapidly!" To the contrary.) With the utmost slowness, until he got the large, sword-shaped handle in his right hand, at first only from above, with his outstretched arm, which he then began gradually to bend, to the same extent that he succeeded in letting his body slide lower; till his arm was finally totally bent, his hand at shoulder-height and hanging on to the handle from below. And now, still with the utmost slowness, he let his body slide lower, first with his midsection lying on the hump, then with his stomach, one foot already dangling in the void, the other still somehow clinging to the rock, as was his whole leg, spread far to the left, especially the inside of his thigh; his left hand and forearm moved from rough spot to rough spot on the rock. Which means: he began to trust more and more of his weight to his right arm, which stretched further and further. If he didn't succeed at the most difficult thing, namely, gaining a foothold underneath the rock-hump and that in an at least vertical position, he would still have this one powerful handle with which to pull himself back up (perhaps gripping it with both hands).

And there, as his right arm was already stretched almost to its limit, this handle — in which, truly, no one could have suspected any malice — this handle gave way, crumbled in his hand.

And that was the end, he fell — as anyone who has gotten a fairly clear idea of this cliff from the description would be bound to assume.

That he didn't fall was due to a millimeter, perhaps, to a few grams of his weight distribution, and most of all to a truly extraordinary talent for climbing.

One thing was clear: the only possibility was to go back up.

But how? Difficult to say — no, impossible to say. Spots of the most extreme difficulty (the so-called sixth degree) — and into such a spot Ull had accidentally landed — are identified by there being no exact instructions for how to master them, and in fact no instructions at all. (At the most: hints.)

Should he try to proceed as quickly as possible? The smallest jerky movement would have meant an immediate fall. A gymnast who pulls himself up effortlessly on the rings with one arm — what would he have accomplished here, with his specialized strength? Absolutely nothing. For where to apply his strength? — To be sure it required extraordinary strength; but a strength divided among countless places. Apart from his right leg, which was dangling in midair, there was hardly a spot on his body that wasn't in use. The foot of his left leg, spread wide and stretching to the other side, which was not yet entirely vertical, sought with its edge a bit of footing—which, however, served only for the least part of his body weight; his inner thigh contributed at least as much through its friction. His extended left hand, though almost fully stretched out, tried to latch on to a protrusion in the rock; it was helped by the friction of his arm, especially his forearm. But his right hand, with his arm still not entirely outstretched, clung, if one could call it that, to the stub that remained of the broken handle, which hardly protruded from the wall at all. And all that together might not have been enough to hold his body; but, added to that, he was clinging to the cliff with his entire front side, as if he had been poured into it. (He would even have used his chin, had it been useful—and possible.)

He had to continue upward—; the only thing worth mentioning about his progress is that it took place almost imperceptibly, and by centimeters—now here, now there. Such difficult climbing—the most difficult climbing—cannot be compared with that of any animal. No need to even mention chamois, since they can't climb at all, though they are far superior to people in getting around, jumping included. With squirrels, which achieve the unheard-of in climbing, one easily forgets their tails, which allow them to use the air—so, in a way, to fly. Monkeys, perhaps? That I don't know. But a comparison from the plant world, with all its diversity, seems inevitable: ivy.

How long it lasted, whether only a number of seconds or minutes or a quarter of an hour, would have been impossible for him to say. But we can assume that the entire undertaking played out in one to two minutes (since no one could have held out longer). Only then, as he had the hump underneath him, and covered the remaining two meters to his earlier position without difficulty, did he hear a roaring sound—but it didn't come from the mountain. It was his breath.

17

THE GIRLFRIEND'S VOICE

When he had reached the safe spot once more, his foot on the platform and his arm looped around the crag as before – then he ceased to know or care, for a while, how his situation looked on the whole; at first only a vague feeling of bliss prevailed.

The heaviness of his breathing gradually subsided, and gradually his eyes opened back up to take in the entirety of his situation – night was falling, and that eliminated the one possibility, namely, to go back to the crest. On what impossible spot would he have to spend the night? On the entire wall there was no match for the one here in security, in "comfort." He could have spent the night here safely, with his body tied, but in what state would he have found himself in the morning? Over there, beyond the couloir, at the foot of the wall that bordered it there, was a place as if made for a bivouac – the only level place since the crest –

a kind of rocky pulpit big enough for several people, only a little bit farther down and from here visible only in profile — but how to get there? He could see no solution.

Or he would have to sacrifice the rope. But farther below, the bergschrund threatened, and under no circumstances could it be conquered without a rope. No solution.

And as he, in the infinite multifariousness of the rock-world, looked hopelessly for help in every direction — help came.

It came from his girlfriend. Hadn't she always been there for him? Hadn't he just lowered her down on the rope, and wasn't she down there now, where the rucksack lay? Meanwhile he heard her voice, close by, very peaceful and warm: "Couldn't you just cut off a little piece of the rope and make a loop out of it?"

That was the solution. That this had not occurred to him — how dazed must he have been! What followed took place very easily. He untied himself (one arm still looped over the crag), cut off a piece about two meters long, tied himself immediately back up (for woe, if the rope had slipped away from him!); knotted a ring out of the cut piece around his rope and laid it around the crag. Then he pulled the rope from below until it was taut, and with the help of the two strands in a matter of moments he was over the difficulty on the easier ground, where his rucksack lay.

But his beloved, who had rescued him? She was no longer there.

Had he really believed she was there? In the deepest part of him, certainly not. But he had heard her voice.

18

THE LONG NIGHT

On a slanted rib leading downward he reached the couloir where it had come out of the ravine and was considerably less steep; this couloir was formed of snow and ice and frequently falling rocks, and it had to be crossed (it ended farther down in smooth cliffs that quickly disappeared from view — a second extension of the large overhang). He managed to cross it, not without a dangerous leap which he would not have risked under different circumstances; now he was again headed diagonally upward, to the long-espied ledge — the pulpit, the rock sofa — just as night fell.

Cliffs are always more complicated than they appear from afar, and every description is necessarily a description from afar (otherwise the description would never end). I say pulpit — but the balustrade was missing. Sofa — but the spot was wider than a sofa and the front side did not break off in a right angle, but rather bent gradually; the back side, however, was gigantically high and overhung the sofa at first; the ground was covered with all kinds of scree and till, and it offered rich opportunity for the night's only, or at least main, activity: clapping his shoes against each other.

It was not very cold, perhaps five degrees below zero, but what was the state of his equipment in terms of a bivouac? There was the thin blanket — otherwise nothing really. (A sleeping bag — a dream!) He put on every piece of clothing he had; it consisted of a second shirt, a jerkin under his thick jacket, another pair of wool socks. He laid the rope, which luckily had remained dry, in loops on the rock so that he could sit on it. The rucksack next to him, now and then behind him, to lay his head on — but not for long. For what everything depended on: his not falling asleep.

At first it was still warm. Especially with his body heat. And all other considerations were no match for the well-being that arose from finally finding a place, after so many hours, where he could rest, even stretch out.

But it quickly got colder. (The elevation was approximately that of the Jungfraujoch.) The sudden falling of ice and rock down through the couloir, however, didn't stop until deep into the night; only near the middle of the night did it slacken.

Clapping his shoe-soles together served three purposes: first, to prevent his feet from freezing; second, to help in the endless battle against falling asleep; and finally, to contribute to overcoming — time, well, if one can say that. He sought to draw out the shoe-clapping to five minutes each time. He also undertook other things to kill the "time": he lit the lantern (a single match sufficed, so still was the night), incidentally, also, to warm his hands, then, after a while, put it out again; he clapped again with his shoes; he smoked his pipe and looked at his watch: almost twenty minutes had gone by. Then he shoved his hands back down deep into his pockets between his pressed-together thighs. He had his hat pulled down on both sides as he had back during the snowstorm. (Back then: when was it? Less than two days ago!)

From time to time he tried to eat, but he succeeded as little as he had from the beginning; after his inhuman efforts, he was overpowered only by thirst. He nibbled on a piece of cheese, on a dried sausage — it could not be called eating; only with the chocolate could he get a bit more down. Then there was still the tiny schnapps bottle, already almost empty; he took a sip and kept the remaining two thimblesful for the next day — for the setting-off.

The felt-covered one-liter canteen, which had been filled in the morning and filled again during the day with snow, was empty. Now, there was certainly plenty of ice and snow around, but these are poor nutrition, and it is very difficult to produce even the smallest amounts of water out of the means available in the high mountains.

– Now he clapped again with the soles of his shoes, five minutes long. He lit the lantern again, his only company; it lit up the nearest surroundings in a friendly way, let the rest sink into the night. He smoked his pipe again and looked at his watch: almost twenty minutes. Then again the seconds, which would eventually turn into a minute; how time can stretch out! How was it to be lived through; where should he begin? Couldn't he shake the night to make it go faster?

To fall asleep, to let himself sink into sleep, what a temptation, again and again! But he couldn't allow himself to, not that, absolutely not.

The moon was insignificant, late risen and not visible from here, recognizable only by the indistinct shadows it cast across the way. The only things that were moving were the stars. Below him, an impenetrable darkness.

But what one saw in the heights, especially a pillar to the right in the same face (it was the southwest crest of the summit, which he ought to have climbed up to), black and apparently fully vertical in front of the starry sky, was monstrously high, higher than one had ever seen. There was no longer any sound, since the crashing of falling rocks had stopped; no sound of rushing water; one no longer heard the roaring of the mountain night. But suddenly a deafening crack, as if a tower had collapsed — and then again dead silence.

The most important matter, the most difficult activity, of this night, was, as already mentioned, the fight against sleep. (For if he had fallen asleep, either he would never have reawakened or he would have awakened in such a state as to make any further action impossible.) And out of this endless struggle he emerged a victor — mostly. For there were tiny moments in which he did fall into a kind of half-sleep; no, however small the moments were, it was real sleep; for he dreamed. Such a dream lasted perhaps only seconds, and then his hard will battered him again from outside.

Thus he suddenly found himself in a warm, familiar chamber, remembering with sympathetic astonishment how he had just fancied himself to be exposed, freezing to the marrow on a narrow strip in a monstrous cliff wall; with the impenetrable blacks of the depths, with cliffs and glaciers jutting into the zenith of the heavens, as if he were caught in the throat of an unimaginably large animal, whose teeth were the towers and corner pillars; the dark abyss was its gullet, the stars its eyes.

And then there were the other moments, that were no longer dreams but a mix of waking and dreaming, exactly what one calls a hallucination. In such a moment he had suddenly found the definitive answer to the oft-asked question: "Why climb a mountain?"

(For all of the usual answers were insufficient: For one's health: but there must certainly be other, and less costly, means for that. For the heights: but what about funicular railways, airplanes? Because it's an especially substantial kind of sport, which, even if only in narrow circles, earns you an especial distinction from an elite: that was better, but also insufficient.) This was it:

To escape from prison.

...And now?

19

THE BERGSCHRUND

Morning came — slowly, but finally it really was light; it brought no joyful deliverance, however, for now new problems emerged. First of all, this: his limbs were almost completely stiff, which made setting off still unthinkable, for crossing the steep stretch of névé going downward, without a pickaxe, demanded a great deal of agility, more precisely flexibility, and indeed the utmost flexibility. So he still had hours to wait, but since the weather was beautiful and hardly any wind was blowing, the temperature rose quickly; and at about seven o'clock he was ready — as ready as one in his situation could be.

Meanwhile, the start of the descent was rendered easier by the fact that the first approximately ten meters could safely be covered on the doubled rope, and with the possibility, should continuing seem inauspicious, of getting back up to the platform easily. (And actually, he could have made such an attempt earlier.)

It was easy to find an appropriate spot, a kind of boulder around which to place the rope. So he climbed down — after he had taken his last sip of schnapps for strength, the last, tiny sip, which he had saved overnight for this occasion. He also ate a bit of snow — poor nourishment. The snow, incidentally — first thin, intermixed with stones and already melting — quickly turned into the compact mass of the névé. This mass was at once hard and soft, or, more precisely: partly hard and partly soft. Arrived at the end of the rope, he stood there a moment in order to think things over thoroughly. He held both ends of the rope in his hands, which would allow him to go back up to the platform again at any time. One leg held all his weight, buried deep and straight in the snow in what seemed to be a very secure foothold, while the other, bent at a right angle, touched the slope much higher up, and actually served only for balance. Underneath him the névé slope dropped away thirty or forty meters more until a seam ran long and straight to left and right, here and there marked by small boulders and other traces of rock, based on which, with a fair degree of certainty, one could expect a bergschrund, probably with a cliff above it; only significantly lower down could the glacier be glimpsed.

Continue down in a straight line? Out of the question. Again he had to think of the chamois. How would a chamois have gotten itself out of this? (Chamois had no pickaxes, either — though, admittedly, four legs.) A chamois would definitely not have descended vertically. — He ruminated, and then formed a plan — the only possible one:

He had to cross the névé slope in a diagonal line, and indeed more horizontally than downward (about two parts horizontal and one part downward). But the following two rules had to be followed with absolute strictness: he had to move with the greatest possible speed (and, where possible, leaping rather than stepping), and in an at least vertical body position; under no circumstances was he to bend toward the mountain.

An extraordinary task for the legs. His arms had nothing to do except provide a small measure of balance.

If he proceeded exactly according to these rules, he ought to make it.

So he started pulling the rope down toward him and collecting it, which required a few lunging movements. While he was thus occupied, he suddenly felt, in one foot, the foot of his standing leg, a murmuring — a very faint, but uncanny feeling... as if something were giving way. Lightning-quick he grabbed instinctively for his pickaxe; but it was... not there. He clawed with his hands in the snow, what else could he do? But in doing so his body fell into a lopsided position parallel to the snow-slope, and the ground gave way fully under his feet. He slid, his hands and arms couldn't stop it; the sliding quickly accelerated; he was whisked to the bergschrund, which was wider and deeper than he could have guessed — and was no more to be seen.

20

THE WILD BROOK

Ull had already long since ventured on his endless battle against the glacier as Johann hurried blithely down the mountain; at least, he seemed blithe. After the snow-slopes, he crossed the alpine terrace and soon reached the same spot where, three days ago, during the first part of the climb, they had rested, and here he sat down once more. The spring was still flowing as it had then, and it was almost the same time of day. Below, the lowlands... the suffocating depths, the hot steam that issued from it... His thoughts went to the other man, whom he'd abandoned, who now, up there, was completing the bold deeds, who perhaps now was already standing upon a peak. (How little true were his imaginings!) He grew sleepy and felt wretched at the same time. All of a sudden he choked and vomited.

He stood up and shook himself — he had to go back down into the lowlands, after all. He hurried through the slope that had seemed so long during the climb up. (All of a sudden he had become a better mountain-climber.) He reached the hamlet — consisting of a few houses, with hardly a human being in sight; there were a few partly flat meadows or fields around it. This area was about fifty to a hundred meters above the bottom of the "side valley" (which, however, seen from here, was temporarily the main valley) and over there, on the other bank, one saw the road leading down it, the road the bus had taken. Only, this bus had set them down a considerable ways higher up in the valley, namely where the footbridge was, and they had arrived here from the opposite direction, down the valley and at the same time climbing upward. Now Johann wanted to take a shortcut to avoid this detour.

So he left the path and went over the fields. He would cross the brook (or tiny river) even without a footbridge, even if it had to be done with a few leaps; there were enough boulders in such a brook; and when not at this spot, then at another. The slope that led down to it, what difficulties could it have to offer? First there were meadows, then a kind of forest, hardly more than two houses high. — Then, suddenly, a farmer somewhere, one or two fields away, with an implement on his shoulder, started walking and making very energetic signals.

"What — forbidden?" Johann called.

"No — but dangerous!"

A monstrous laugh, not unlike the neighing of a horse, was the answer. — *He* had to be told, *him*, a high-alpinist! What did such a hare-brained little farmer have to tell *him* about danger — a simple little farmer, who'd surely never gotten beyond the alpine meadows — what did he know about the ice storms up there?

A high-alpinist! Or at least, the companion of a real high-alpinist, whom he had abandoned — but that didn't count right now: he belonged to it: to the realm of the heights, not of the depths. So, already in the lowlands, he took possession of something from his having been with Ull that expressed itself as arrogance — insolence even. Ull himself would never have answered the farmer's advice with such contempt.

Johann continued on his way, more determined than before. The meadow slanted and turned into a forest of an unusual kind: the fir trees stood far apart from each other, but they were the only things that offered a safe purchase; between them were plants that completely covered the ground. These plants, obviously related to rhubarb but with much thinner and longer stalks, formed a complete roof with their leaves; but the ground, which wasn't visible, offered his feet only poor purchase and even the pickaxe couldn't help much (precisely because nothing under the leaf-roof could be seen); this ground, namely, was made of very little wet earth or loam and predominantly out of ledge, over which water trickled. Suddenly Johann's feet began to slide; no tree was within reach; he grabbed for the plants, which came out in his hands and accompanied him into the deeps; so he was whisked into the brook and hit his head against a rock.

Was it a brook or a small river? As you like; or, rather: farther down in the valley, where it became wider and flatter, one would indeed have to speak of a small river; but here it was a torrential mountain brook. It didn't conduct a large amount of water; but this water came around with violent strength now from the left, now from the right, around boulders, which offered either no purchase or not enough purchase, because too slippery or too round; Johann was already hurtled farther into the hiss, head down, head up, hitting a rock, then, resisting, hitting another rock, gurgling and moaning in deeper water again (for there were also holes one or two meters deep); so — without one being able to say how much the blows to his head and how much the water itself contributed to it — he quickly perished.

88   And this quickness is striking. Because of its contradiction to the manner in which he lived his life, in which almost everything had unfolded with melancholy slowness. — And Ull's end, which, reckoned at the latest from the loss of the pickaxe, lasted about twenty-four hours; or, if one multiplies the night hours spent on the pulpit in the frozen cliffs by ten (for, after all, time has different lengths), more than a hundred hours: did this not also stand in great contrast to his nature, his general behavior? So, in their deaths, the two had exchanged roles; and the perhaps senseless question arises, whether the same could not have happened, at least in some small measure — while they lived?

The Swiss author Ludwig Hohl (1904–1980) lived much of his life in relative obscurity, tasting success only in the last decade of his life, when he won, among other prizes, the Robert Walser Centenary Prize (1978). He is best known for his 832-page opus *Die Notizen* (The Notes). He began the novella *Bergfahrt* (*Ascent*) in 1926, revised it repeatedly, then left the manuscript for thirty years before returning to it and giving it its final form. It was first published in 1975.

Donna Stonecipher is the author of three books of poetry, most recently *The Cosmopolitan* (Coffee House Press, 2008).

Thank you to the Swiss Society of New York,
the Max Geilinger-Stiftung, Pro Helvetia, and
Canton Glarus for helping to make
this publication possible.

Swiss Society
of New York

swiss arts council

SWISSLOS
Lotteriefonds
Kanton Glarus

Ascent is composed in Adobe Jenson. One thousand copies have been printed and bound by Thomson-Shore Printers in Dexter, Michigan.